THE TALE
OF
THE FLOPSY BUNNIES

THE TALE OF
THE FLOPSY BUNNIES

BY

BEATRIX POTTER

Author of
"The Tale of Peter Rabbit." &c.

BLOOMSBURY BOOKS
in association with
FREDERICK WARNE

FOR ALL LITTLE FRIENDS
OF
MR. McGREGOR & PETER & BENJAMIN

8

IT is said that the effect of eating too much lettuce is " soporific."

I have never felt sleepy after eating lettuces; but then *I* am not a rabbit.

They certainly had a very soporific effect upon the Flopsy Bunnies!

WHEN Benjamin Bunny grew up, he married his Cousin Flopsy. They had a large family, and they were very improvident and cheerful.

I do not remember the separate names of their children; they were generally called the "Flopsy Bunnies."

12

AS there was not always quite enough to eat,—Benjamin used to borrow cabbages from Flopsy's brother, Peter Rabbit, who kept a nursery garden.

SOMETIMES Peter Rabbit
had no cabbages to spare.

15

16

WHEN this happened, the Flopsy Bunnies went across the field to a rubbish heap, in the ditch outside Mr. McGregor's garden.

MR. McGREGOR'S rubbish heap was a mixture. There were jam pots and paper bags, and mountains of chopped grass from the mowing machine (which always tasted oily), and some rotten vegetable marrows and an old boot or two. One day—oh joy !—there were a quantity of overgrown lettuces, which had " shot " into flower.

19

THE Flopsy Bunnies simply stuffed lettuces. By degrees, one after another, they were overcome with slumber, and lay down in the mown grass.

Benjamin was not so much overcome as his children. Before going to sleep he was sufficiently wide awake to put a paper bag over his head to keep off the flies.

THE little Flopsy Bunnies slept delightfully in the warm sun. From the lawn beyond the garden came the distant clacketty sound of the mowing machine. The blue-bottles buzzed about the wall, and a little old mouse picked over the rubbish among the jam pots.

(I can tell you her name, she was called Thomasina Tittle-mouse, a woodmouse with a long tail.)

23

24

SHE rustled across the paper bag, and awakened Benjamin Bunny.

The mouse apologized profusely, and said that she knew Peter Rabbit.

WHILE she and Benjamin were talking, close under the wall, they heard a heavy tread above their heads ; and suddenly Mr. McGregor emptied out a sackful of lawn mowings right upon the top of the sleeping Flopsy Bunnies ! Benjamin shrank down under his paper bag. The mouse hid in a jam pot.

27

28

THE little rabbits smiled sweetly in their sleep under the shower of grass; they did not awake because the lettuces had been so soporific.

They dreamt that their mother Flopsy was tucking them up in a hay bed.

Mr. McGregor looked down after emptying his sack. He saw some funny little brown tips of ears sticking up through the lawn mowings. He stared at them for some time.

PRESENTLY a fly settled on one of them and it moved.

Mr. McGregor climbed down on to the rubbish heap—

" One, two, three, four ! five ! six leetle rabbits! " said he as he dropped them into his sack. The Flopsy Bunnies dreamt that their mother was turning them over in bed. They stirred a little in their sleep, but still they did not wake up.

31

32

MR. McGREGOR tied up the sack and left it on the wall.

He went to put away the mowing machine.

WHILE he was gone, Mrs. Flopsy Bunny (who had remained at home) came across the field.

She looked suspiciously at the sack and wondered where everybody was?

35

36

THEN the mouse came out of her jam pot, and Benjamin took the paper bag off his head, and they told the doleful tale.

Benjamin and Flopsy were in despair, they could not undo the string.

But Mrs. Tittlemouse was a resourceful person. She nibbled a hole in the bottom corner of the sack.

THE little rabbits were pulled out and pinched to wake them.

Their parents stuffed the empty sack with three rotten vegetable marrows, an old blacking-brush and two decayed turnips.

40

THEN they all hid under a bush and watched for Mr. McGregor.

M^{R.} McGREGOR came back and picked up the sack, and carried it off.

He carried it hanging down, as if it were rather heavy.

The Flopsy Bunnies followed at a safe distance.

43

44

THEY watched him go into
his house.

And then they crept up to
the window to listen.

M^{R.} McGREGOR threw down the sack on the stone floor in a way that would have been extremely painful to the Flopsy Bunnies, if they had happened to have been inside it.

They could hear him drag his chair on the flags, and chuckle—

" One, two, three, four, five, six leetle rabbits ! " said Mr. McGregor.

47

48

" EH ? What's that ? What have they been spoiling now ? " enquired Mrs. McGregor.

" One, two, three, four, five, six leetle fat rabbits ! " repeated Mr. McGregor, counting on his fingers—"one, two, three—"

" Don't you be silly ; what do you mean, you silly old man ? "

" In the sack ! one, two, three, four, five, six ! " replied Mr. McGregor.

(The youngest Flopsy Bunny got upon the window-sill.)

MRS. McGREGOR took hold of the sack and felt it. She said she could feel six, but they must be *old* rabbits, because they were so hard and all different shapes.

"Not fit to eat; but the skins will do fine to line my old cloak."

"Line your old cloak?" shouted Mr. McGregor—"I shall sell them and buy myself baccy!"

"Rabbit tobacco! I shall skin them and cut off their heads."

52

MRS. McGREGOR untied the sack and put her hand inside.

When she felt the vegetables she became very very angry. She said that Mr. McGregor had " done it a purpose."

AND Mr. McGregor was very angry too. One of the rotten marrows came flying through the kitchen window, and hit the youngest Flopsy Bunny.

It was rather hurt.

THEN Benjamin and Flopsy
thought that it was time
to go home.

58

SO Mr. McGregor did not get his tobacco, and Mrs. McGregor did not get her rabbit skins.

But next Christmas Thomasina Tittlemouse got a present of enough rabbit-wool to make herself a cloak and a hood, and a handsome muff and a pair of warm mittens.